The War
MONKEY

For my parents,
who saw it all through children's eyes.
With love, C.F.

The WAR Monkey

Claire Funge

Illustrated by Peter Bailey

OXFORD
UNIVERSITY PRESS

OXFORD

UNIVERSITY PRESS

Great Clarendon Street, Oxford OX2 6DP

Oxford University Press is a department of the University of Oxford.
It furthers the University's objective of excellence in research, scholarship,
and education by publishing worldwide in

Oxford   New York

Auckland   Cape Town   Dar es Salaam   Hong Kong   Karachi
Kuala Lumpur   Madrid   Melbourne   Mexico City   Nairobi
New Delhi   Shanghai   Taipei   Toronto

With offices in

Argentina   Austria   Brazil   Chile   Czech Republic   France   Greece
Guatemala   Hungary   Italy   Japan   Poland   Portugal   Singapore
South Korea   Switzerland   Thailand   Turkey   Ukraine   Vietnam

Oxford is a registered trade mark of Oxford University Press
in the UK and in certain other countries

Text © Claire Funge 2001

The moral rights of the author have been asserted

Database right Oxford University Press (maker)

First published 2001
This edition 2005

British Library Cataloguing in Publication Data
Data available

ISBN-13: 978-0-19-918461-3
ISBN-10: 0-19-918461-5

3 5 7 9 10 8 6 4 2

Available in packs
Stage 16 More Stories A Pack of 6:
ISBN-13: 978-0-19-918446-0; ISBN-10: 0-19-918446-1
Stage 16 More Stories A Class Pack:
ISBN-13: 978-0-19-918463-7; ISBN-10: 0-19-918463-1
Guided Reading Cards also available:
ISBN-13: 978-0-19-918465-1; ISBN-10: 0-19-918465-8

Cover artwork by Peter Sutton

Printed in Great Britain by
Ashford Colour Press, Gosport Hants

Contents

Prologue

The sound of a mug being placed on her bedside table gently roused Tegan from her sleep.

'Cup of tea, love. It's time to get up.'

The footsteps had left the room before Tegan was awake enough to let her dad know she had heard him. So she stayed in her nest, relishing that cosy feeling when you're neither asleep nor awake and your mind isn't really working. Gradually the noises of the day began to cut their way through and Tegan rolled over and her eyelids fluttered open.

'Dreams,' she thought, 'are funny things.' But then, as she reached out for the mug she heard a cry, a baby's cry, and she froze.

Tegan heard Mum in the next room. 'It must be real. She must be home already,' thought Tegan.

'Aww, Kit,' she heard Mum say gently. 'It's OK, I'm here.' The cries turned to snuffling sounds. Mum must have picked him up.

Tegan lay back on her pillow and tried to piece things together. It *wasn't* a dream, Kit was real. 'But does that mean that all of it was real?' she wondered. 'What happened at Nanna's?' Questions came to her thick and fast but Tegan pushed them away. It was all too strange and far too scary to think about.

Mum came into the room with a tiny baby in her arms. He was quiet now. She sat down on the edge of Tegan's bed.

'Hello, love. This is Kit,' she said, tilting the bundle in her arms towards Tegan. 'Kit, I'd like you to meet your big sister – Tegan.'

Kit gurgled.

'Is it good to be home?' asked Mum, kissing Tegan's forehead. Tegan nodded. So Nanna's hadn't been a dream. She reached out and stroked Kit's teeny hand.

'I still can't believe I've got a brother,' she said. 'But I think that I'm going to like it. Until he can walk and talk anyway! Then he'll be banned from my bedroom,' Tegan laughed.

'Kit,' she said, testing out his name. 'Hello, Kit, Kitten.'

Tegan's mum stood up with the sleeping Kit and went to leave.

'Would you like to send Nanna some flowers as a thank you?'

'Yes, definitely,' replied Tegan.

As soon as Mum had gone, Tegan pulled out her special shoe-box. There was the framed photograph lying on the top. She'd only put it in there yesterday. Treating it with great care, as though it might vanish from her hands, she scanned the black and white photograph inside. It still looked the same. There was her grandmother, aged about twenty, sitting on the beach at Weymouth with Tegan's great-grandparents. But just as she was about to put it back in the box, Tegan noticed something cut off one side of the photograph, hiding behind the frame edge.

Her fingers fumbled with the little metal catches on the back and the photograph and the glass holding it in place fell into her lap. Tegan reached for the picture and lifted it up close, her eyes darting from side to side. There, hidden behind the wooden edge of the frame she found what she had been looking for.

Another girl. But was it who she thought it was?

CHAPTER 1

Family secrets

Nanna's house was a large, red-brick villa in west London. Tegan didn't know it well. She had lived in Australia until she was seven as her mum and dad had emigrated when she was still a baby.

Tegan liked it in Australia and she'd really missed her friends when she arrived in Britain in the middle of a cold, wet winter four years ago. But Mum and Dad were much happier here. 'A Fresh Start,' Dad called it when they settled down in Devon. Tegan liked Devon. She liked it more the longer she lived there and now she had lots of friends. They didn't even notice her Australian accent any more. Besides, it was fading fast these days. And Dad always said she could go back to Australia when she was older if she wanted to.

Devon was a long way from London. So, although Nanna came down to see them at least three times a year, Tegan had only visited the house in London once before. It had been at Christmas a couple of years ago. They'd had a great time. Tegan had gone to see the lights in Oxford Street and gone window shopping in Hamleys.

Nanna had said she was going to give her a Christmas like the ones she'd had as a child, living in that same house. She'd found Tegan an old stocking and put the traditional old penny, orange and a walnut in it, along with pretty pink sugared mice and a stick of liquorice. Tegan had loved it, especially as she had her pillowcase full of presents to open as well.

Now, two years later, it was the Easter school holidays and Tegan was back for a whole week. Mum was having a baby. A brother or sister for

Tegan was all part of their 'Fresh Start'. It had taken longer than expected, but now it was all systems go and Mum was due to go into hospital a few days before the birth. Nothing to worry about, they told her. But with Dad at work all day, Tegan had been asked if she'd rather go to her friend Katie's, or to Nanna's. After much thought she'd opted for Nanna's. Katie was a lot of fun, but she could also be rather bossy.

And London might be exciting. Perhaps she would get to visit Madame Tussaud's and Hollywood Galaxy Cafe this time?

It was Sunday afternoon when the car pulled up outside the house after a journey of nearly five hours. Tegan was glad they had finally arrived. The large wooden door with stained-glass panels opened and Nanna stood there beaming at them.

'Good journey?' she called as Tegan pushed open the car door.

'Hello, Nanna. Yes, thanks,' she replied, smiling.

Dad took out Tegan's hold-all then followed her up the path. He only stayed for a quick cup of tea before making the return journey, as he wanted to try and make it to the hospital before visiting time was over.

'Give Mum lots of love,' said Tegan.

'I will, and I'll call you tonight,' said Dad, lifting Tegan off her feet as she kissed him goodbye.

* * *

Tegan and Nanna sat down for their first tea together. Nanna had made toasted cheese and ham sandwiches and, as a special first-night treat, there was chocolate-chip ice-cream for dessert.

'My absolute favourite,' said Tegan.

'When I was your age, there was still rationing after the war. You'd never believe what we went without in those days.'

'Like what?' asked Tegan, as she took a large bite from her toastie.

'Sweets were rationed and so was chocolate. But we did get the odd stick of chewing gum from the American soldiers during the war. Everything was in short supply. No bananas. I was older than you are when I remember tasting my first one. I didn't know how to eat it and tried to take a bite with the skin still on.'

Tegan giggled.

'But wasn't it exciting, too?' asked Tegan. 'I mean, all the planes and air raids and bombed-out houses to play in?' Tegan had been learning about the war at school and thought it sounded like a great adventure.

Nanna took Tegan's empty plate and went over to the sink. 'It was at the beginning, but when people you knew started getting hurt, it grew frightening. This kitchen we're sitting in now is newer than the rest of this house. It used to be an old kitchen and scullery when I was young. But one night a bomb landed at the top of the street. It took our kitchen with it.'

Nanna paused for a moment before adding, 'It took my sister, Alice, too.'

Tegan was puzzled. 'Alice?' she said. 'I didn't know you had a sister called Alice.'

'Well, maybe that's a story for another time,' said Nanna, going to the freezer to get the ice-cream.

But Tegan couldn't let Nanna get away without telling the full story. 'Please, Nanna, tell me about her. What happened?'

Nanna came back and sat down. 'I suppose you're old enough to know. Besides, it's all such a long time ago.

'It was in 1945, the last year of the war. I was ten and Alice was five.

'It was early evening when the air-raid siren went, which meant we all had to go down to the Anderson shelter for the night. The old thing's still there. I use it as a garden shed now. You can go and have a look inside tomorrow if you want. Anyway, it was a scramble as usual to get coats on and everyone together.

'We were near the bottom of the garden when Alice suddenly shouted, 'Monkey. I haven't got Monkey.' And she ran as fast as she could towards the house. Alice never went anywhere without her Monkey. He used to be lovely and fluffy, but Alice loved him so much that he was totally threadbare in places.

'In the dark and with the noise of the planes droning overhead it was a few moments before anyone realized she had gone. My mother dropped everything she was carrying and chased after her. But the bomb landed. It was a Doodlebug.

'I'd never seen anything like it in my life. I stood rooted to the spot in the entrance to the Anderson shelter as half the houses in our street were swept clean away. They just disappeared in clouds of smoke and dust, taking our kitchen with them. Alice was caught in the blast. She had nearly made it to the kitchen door when she was blown off her feet. And all for a furry toy monkey.'

Nanna paused, lost in the past. 'So that's what

happened to Alice.'

Tegan was silent for a few seconds. 'That's very sad,' she said finally, in a quiet voice.

'That's wars for you,' said Nanna, standing up and breaking the solemn mood.

'Did you ever find the monkey?' asked Tegan.

'No,' said Nanna. 'The monkey went along with Alice. Now, enough of the war. It was all a long time ago. Why don't we go upstairs and sort out your room?'

Tegan smiled. 'OK,' she said. But she knew that she wanted to know more.

CHAPTER 2

The Anderson Shelter

Next morning, Nanna was already out in the garden, tending to her vegetable patch when Tegan came downstairs. Tegan knocked on the window to get her attention and waved, then she settled herself down in front of the portable TV with a bowl of cereal.

Nanna poked her head around the kitchen door. 'It's a lovely day. Come and help me, if you like.'

Tegan wasn't entirely sure she did want to help. Digging vegetables didn't sound like much fun. Maybe she should have gone to Katie's after all. But, so as not to disappoint Nanna, she smiled back. 'Sure. I'll be out soon.'

'Then,' added Nanna, 'what about a trip into town? We could go to Hollywood Galaxy Cafe for lunch if you like.'

Tegan beamed. 'Great,' she said. Now that was more like it.

Tegan wandered out into the garden. She'd thought a lot about what Nanna had told her last night. She tried to imagine what it had been like living in this house during the war, but it was just too difficult. Everything was different now. Everybody was different.

It was a long garden, with lots of places for dens. It was a shame Katie wasn't with her now, there were some great spots to hold secret club meetings. At the bottom of the garden was the Anderson shelter. It was made of corrugated metal, painted green, with just the large dome of its roof sticking out of the lawn. The rest of it was sunk into the earth. There were a few steep steps down from ground level.

Tegan carefully went down them and stood facing the door. A shiver of anticipation ran through her as she reached for the bolt on the outside. She knew it was only a garden shed, but after all she had learned last night, it had become more than that. This shed had been exactly where it was now, on that night the bomb landed and Alice was killed.

Nanna, who was up the garden merrily digging away, had stood exactly where Tegan was now, as she saw the bomb land at the end of the street. Tegan turned around to see the view for herself. But there was a clear blue sky above her and the only plane in sight was a passenger jet way, way up in the clouds.

Tegan eased the bolt back. It was stiff, obviously nobody had been in the shelter for a while. She worked at it for a few seconds before it released the door and she could peer inside. At first, Tegan couldn't see anything. The light was so strong outside and the shelter so dark inside she had to wait for her eyes to adjust. Tegan wasn't sure what she had been expecting, but what she saw was rather a disappointment. It was, after all, just a garden shed. There were spades, a lawnmower, a bag of peat, all heaped on top of each other. There was a thin pathway down the centre, so as to be able to reach the things at the back.

Tegan took a step inside, letting go of the door, which slammed shut with a clang of metal on metal behind her. Panicking in the pitch dark, she quickly opened it, letting in light and air and, finding a box in the corner, wedged it against the door to keep it open.

She had hoped that the shelter might hold some kind of secret to life in the war. But it was just an old, worn-out relic, full of cobwebs and dirty garden things. Nanna was right, the war was a long time ago.

Tegan picked up the box she had been using to wedge the door open. She was about to throw it back into the shed when she noticed something written on the outside. The writing was in faded scrawly black ink, so scrawly Tegan could hardly make it out. She peered at it, forcing her eyes to make sense of the letters.

'Al, alee . . . aleec,' she muttered out loud. And then it dawned on her just what the word was: 'Alice'.

'Alice,' Tegan almost shouted. Now she could see. 'Alice Wilkinson.'

Tegan's fingers started to tremble as she desperately tried to open the box. Within seconds she was holding something black and rubbery with straps, a clear visor thing with a funny nozzle on one side. Tegan realized what it was. 'Her gas mask,' she said out loud.

Tegan turned it round in her hands excitedly. It was old and dirty, but it was a real link with the past. Not only that, but it had belonged to Alice. Tegan began to wonder whether the last person ever to have seen it or touched it was Alice, all those years ago. 'It must have been awful having to wear these things,' she thought.

Tegan was about to go out and show Nanna what she had found, when on impulse, and feeling rather self-conscious, she decided to try it on. She untangled and adjusted the straps. 'After all, it was made to fit a five-year-old,' she thought.

Tegan bent her head down and pulled it on over her face. She used her hand to wipe away the dirt from the visor and as she did so she realized with mounting apprehension that something very strange had happened. Tegan looked out of the visor to see that the shelter no longer looked like a garden shed. She quickly looked from left to right, expecting any moment for the lawnmower and bag of peat to reappear. But instead, what she saw were little wooden bunk-beds covered in blankets, lining both sides. And the ceiling, which Tegan remembered as a dirty rusty colour, was neatly painted white.

Panic flooded through her, the smell of the old rubber mask began to burn inside her nostrils and she could hear her own heavy breathing inside the mask. She tore it off, gulping for air. And as she did so, Tegan realized that the shelter was once again a garden shed. Everything was back where it should be. Tegan stood still for a few moments, trying to calm down.

'What just happened?' she wondered as she looked down at the mask still in her shaking hands. After a moment, she very gingerly lifted it up to look through the visor, without actually putting it on again. As the visor covered her

eyes, so the shelter changed again and the bunk-beds came into view. She whipped it away again and the shed returned once more.

Gradually, as her confidence grew, Tegan tried it several more times. Each time, as soon as the visor was in front of her eyes, so too was the shelter with its beds. And each time she took it away, the garden shed returned. Tegan realized, with growing excitement, that in looking through the mask she could see the shelter as it was in wartime.

'Am I looking at the past?' she wondered. 'Can I really travel through time?'

Tegan sat down on the bag of peat to think. Now that she knew all she had to do was take the mask off when she wanted to be back in the present, she was itching to have another go and see if the wartime world would extend beyond the Anderson shelter.

But there were a few things which Tegan wasn't sure about. Like how much time would she lose in the present? Would she get back and find that she'd lost days and Nanna was frantic with worry and had the police out looking for her? Or would something happen in the past to stop her getting back again?

There was only one way to find out. Tegan carefully put the gas mask back on, properly this time, because she was intending to stay for a while.

CHAPTER 3

Chrissie

The shelter was much more comfortable than Tegan had expected. The beds looked cosy and there were old books and comics lying on top of one of the bunks. 'I wish it was still like this in the present,' thought Tegan. 'Then I really *would* have a great den!'

She let her eyes wander around, making sure not to miss any details. Tegan knew she would want to remember everything, just in case it never happened again.

The smell of damp began to seep in through the rubbery smell of the mask and Tegan looked down. There were large puddles all over the bare earth floor. 'Maybe this isn't so comfortable after all!' she thought, as the dirty, cold water began to soak through her trainers. Tegan decided that the time had come to venture outside.

'It's now or never,' she thought. She eased open the door and made her way up the familiar steps outside. It was good to be out in the fresh air and away from the dark, dank insides of the shelter. Then Tegan realized why the air suddenly felt so fresh. She lifted her hands up and immediately touched her nose. The mask was no longer on her face. The same panic she had felt after the first time she'd put on the mask, rose in her. And with it came the sheer terror of realizing that without the mask, she was stuck in the past. The mask was the key and she no longer had it! Tegan wrenched open the shelter door and dived back inside, hoping beyond hope that maybe it was still in there. She frantically pulled at blankets and sheets on the beds in a desperate attempt to find it. The comics were tossed to the ground, where they landed in puddles of muddy water, ruined.

Then, in her frenzy, it suddenly dawned on Tegan that she could hear the sound of her own breathing again. Was the mask, in fact, back on her face? Tegan put her hands up to her head and felt its solid rubber form. It was there. It was all right. And slowly she sank on to one of the dishevelled beds in relief. Time was playing tricks on her and she didn't know what the rules were.

'Maybe I should just forget it. This is all getting too dangerous,' she thought.

But a nagging voice in Tegan's head told her that this was something special and she should trust it. She should trust her instincts and follow it through.

After a moment spent regaining her calm, Tegan went up the steps of the shelter once more and before even reaching the top, she didn't need to touch her face to know that the mask had disappeared again.

'It's OK,' she kept telling herself. 'You'll be OK. You can go back any time you like. Besides,' she thought, 'who is to say that I'm not already back in the present? Time travel might not work outside the shelter.'

But it only took Tegan a second or two to know that she was indeed still in the past. Her eyes scanned the garden. It was roughly the same shape, but there were none of Nanna's carefully tended flower borders. There was no Nanna, either. Now, there were rows and rows of vegetables, taking over most of the garden. Tegan turned to look at the shelter and instead of seeing its green-painted roof, she found that it too was under a layer of earth and had vegetables growing on top! Tegan cast her eyes towards the house.

'Maybe', she thought, 'it's time I went and had a look around.'

As Tegan neared the back of the house, she found that it was different. The door had moved. Then she remembered what Nanna had said about the kitchen being rebuilt.

'That means that I must be in a time *before* the bomb was dropped,' she thought.

Tegan put her hand on the door knob, but withdrew it with a start when she heard voices coming from inside. Tegan stood rooted to the spot. She hadn't stopped to think there might be people around. It simply hadn't crossed her mind. 'Will they be able to see me? Speak to me?' Tegan wondered. And then came the thought that really made the colour drain from her face and her heart start pounding. 'Am I about to find my own family from the past behind this door?'

Before she had time to think any further, the knob turned from the inside and Tegan found herself staring at a girl about the same age as herself.

'Who are you?' said the girl. Tegan's voice failed her. Her lips moved but no sounds came out. She cleared her throat, all the time looking at the girl. She was blond, with her hair cut in a bob and a little slide holding back her fringe. But it was her clothes that Tegan really noticed. She had on a tartan kilt, knee-high socks and a skimpy hand-knitted jumper, which had a few small holes in the welt. Tegan realized how strange she must look to the girl, in her khaki trousers, her favourite flowery top and the long ethnic hair braid she'd had put in by a girl at the beach in Sidmouth the other week.

Tegan was about to speak when she heard an older voice say: 'Who is it, Chrissie?' And a woman appeared behind the girl at the door.

'Hello, love, what can we do for you?' said the woman.

'I . . .' Tegan willed her mind to come up with something fast. 'I've just moved here,' she managed at last.

'That's a funny accent,' said the girl. 'And your clothes are funny, too.'

Suddenly Tegan had an idea, one she hoped they'd believe, although she wasn't too sure on her facts.

'I'm . . . American,' she said, hoping they hadn't heard enough Australian accents to be able to tell the difference. 'My father's posted here,' she continued, her confidence growing as she came out with the biggest lie of her life. 'He was working in England before the war and he's just moved to one of the American camps near here. Mum and I were with him before war broke out and we never went back to the States in time.'

Tegan looked at them expectantly, waiting for them to find a huge mistake in what she'd just said. But instead the woman just opened the door a little wider for Tegan to enter. 'Well, you'd best come in now you're here. This war never stops throwing surprises at you, that's for sure.'

Tegan stepped inside.

'What's your name?' asked Chrissie.

'Tegan,' Tegan replied.

'Funny name, too,' laughed Chrissie.

Tegan was relieved that Chrissie had smiled at last. Then she thought how stupid she was not to have called herself something old-fashioned, like Janet, instead.

The kitchen was dark and Tegan thought it looked rather shabby. There was an enamel sink in one corner and a large, heavy wooden table and chairs standing on an old rag rug. Tegan noticed that there were funny sticky-tape crosses on every pane of glass in the windows and remembered that she'd been told at school how that was done in wartime to stop glass from shattering when bombs landed nearby. As she cast her eyes around the room, a younger girl walked in. Her hair was darker than Chrissie's and it was braided into two plaits. She was

wearing a dark brown pinafore dress. She stopped suddenly when she saw Tegan.

'Alice, this is Tegan. She's American and her father works at the American camp. You and Chrissie will have another playmate, which is nice. Especially as so many of your friends have been evacuated,' said the woman.

Tegan suddenly realized that Chrissie was, of course, short for Christine. Christine was her grandmother's name. Tegan stared at the girl as she realized she had been talking to her own grandmother. And this was Alice, *the* Alice, and she was very much alive!

CHAPTER 4

Alice

Tegan didn't know what to say. More than anything she wanted to tell them the truth. She wanted to tell Chrissie that she'd never believe it but she was her granddaughter. That she'd come all the way from the future and that Chrissie would one day have a daughter called Tessa who was her mum and wasn't it amazing?

But then Tegan thought of what she would have to tell them about Alice and her excitement waned. It was a crazy idea anyway and they'd never believe her.

Tegan noticed that Alice was holding

something furry. 'Who's that you've got, Alice?' she asked with a smile, trying to make friends.

Alice looked at her uncertainly. 'Monkey,' she said. Tegan hadn't been expecting her answer and the smile dropped from her lips.

'Can I have a look at him?' she asked, stretching out her arm towards Alice, who at the mention of Monkey's name had clasped him tightly to her.

'Alice is such a baby,' teased Chrissie. Then putting on a whiny voice she started chanting to Alice, 'Monkey, Monkey. Where's Monkey? Does baby Alice need her little Monkey?'

'Stop it, Chrissie,' said her mother in a voice so stern that it made them all jump.

'Can I look?' asked Tegan again, in the gentlest voice she could manage.

Alice reluctantly handed Monkey over.

'He's very sweet,' Tegan said, more to break the silence than anything else. Tegan held Monkey in her hands. He looked like he had been well loved. His ears were threadbare and his coat, which must once have been fluffy, had matted into bobbles. It made Tegan wonder how old he was. He certainly wasn't new. So how much longer did he have to go before that fateful night? She remembered Nanna's words, how she had said that Monkey was threadbare when it happened. Tegan stared at him, thinking about how what she held in her hands had changed all their lives.

Alice reached out for him.

Tegan decided she had to think of a way to find out what year she was in. 'But how can I just ask?' she thought.

An idea struck her and she turned to Chrissie.

'I'm eleven,' she said. 'How old are you two?'

'I'm ten,' said Chrissie. 'And Alice is five.'

Tegan knew immediately what this meant. It had to be either 1944 or early 1945. Time must be running out for Alice.

Chrissie broke her thoughts.

'What's it like in America?' she said.

The question took Tegan by surprise. How did she know what it was like in America? She'd never set foot in the place. And American films weren't going to help her much when most of those she'd seen were set in the present!

'It's . . . cool,' she said, searching for an American word.

'You mean it's cold?' asked Chrissie's mother.

'Not really,' said Tegan, thrusting her hands deep into her pockets in her embarrassment.

As she did so Tegan felt something hard. It was the half-eaten packet of fruit gums she'd had on the journey yesterday. She pulled them out.

'Would you like one?' she said to Chrissie, holding out the packet in an attempt to change the subject from America.

Chrissie and Alice both shrieked.

'Where did they come from?' asked Chrissie excitedly as she took one. 'I've never seen sweets like these before.'

'They're American,' said Tegan, knowing full well that they were nothing of the kind. But she had no other way of explaining how she'd got them.

'Here, you can keep them,' she said. 'I must be getting back. My mum will be wondering where I've got to.'

Chrissie's mother showed her to the door while Chrissie and Alice still marvelled over the sweets. Thankfully, it was the back door, or Tegan didn't know how she would have made it back to the shelter in the garden.

'Come again,' said the woman who Tegan now knew was her great-grandmother. 'It'll be nice for our Chrissie to have a friend around. So many have left London.'

'I will,' said Tegan. And she hoped she meant it.

Tegan went warily up the garden, taking care not to be spotted from the window. When she was sure that she wouldn't be seen, she quickly scurried down the steps and into the shelter. Before she had even shut the door behind her, she could hear her breathing coming from behind the gas mask. She raised her hands to take it off. But before she did so she had one last look around the wartime shelter, just in case this was all a dream and she'd never see it again. Then she whipped the mask off and found herself standing in the middle of the garden shed. The lawnmower and the garden tools were all back in place.

Tegan carefully put the gas mask back in its box. Then she looked around for a good place to hide it, before deciding on a high shelf at the back.

'It should be OK here,' she reasoned.

Then she sat back down on the bag of peat.

'I won't tell Nanna,' she thought. 'She'd never believe me. But I wonder if I asked her about an American girl whether she would remember?'

Tegan thought about this for a moment or two but then decided to keep quiet. It was too soon. She had to get things straight in her own mind first.

'Tegan, are you still in there?' It was Nanna.

'Oh no!' thought Tegan. 'How long have I been gone?'

Suddenly, she panicked. She felt like she had been caught misbehaving. What if she'd been gone for hours? Tegan looked down at her watch.

'Eleven-thirty,' she said out loud. But then she realized that didn't tell her much because she'd forgotten to look at it before she put the mask on. 'You stupid thing,' she said to herself. 'If you're going to go time travelling, you've got to start thinking about these things, or you're going to find yourself in some serious trouble.'

The door opened and Nanna peered at her from the doorway.

'There you are,' she said. 'Are you going to give me a hand or daydream the day away?'

Tegan smiled at her. 'Phew!' she thought. 'Nanna doesn't seem to think I've been gone very long.'

And she followed Nanna out into the garden.

It was good to be back in the twenty-first century. She smiled when she saw the flower borders where only minutes before there had been vegetables.

'You start at that end and I'll start at this,' said Nanna. 'But no seedlings, only weeds!'

Tegan bent down to begin her work. She had

a grin on her face that she was glad was hidden by her bent head, or Nanna would want to know why it was there. 'So this is Chrissie,' she thought. 'This is the girl who seemed pretty much like me.'

* * *

The bus into town was packed and, when they arrived at Hollywood Galaxy Cafe, Tegan saw to her dismay that there was a queue stretching right round the side of the building. She thought that Nanna might suggest they go somewhere else instead, but she simply walked to the back of the queue and said, 'It looks like we might be here for a while, doesn't it?'

Tegan was finding it hard not to keep looking at Nanna. She couldn't get her head around the idea that this person, who she knew of as Nanna, was also Chrissie, in her kilt and skimpy jumper. As they stood together, Tegan took Nanna's hand in hers.

'I thought queuing for food was finished after the war and rationing stopped,' said Nanna.

Tegan was glad that Nanna was talking about the war again without being prompted. She wanted to know as much as possible about life then, so that she would be ready for going back next time. If there was a 'next time'.

'What did you and Alice do when you were stuck in the shelter?' asked Tegan. She couldn't imagine night after night in the space of the shed with no TV, no computer games, not even a radio.

'We read and talked,' said Nanna. 'And don't forget it was mostly night time, so we tried to get some sleep when the planes would let us. Alice used to sing sometimes. She loved doing that. Only it kept the rest of us awake!' Nanna paused. 'Still, no sense in thinking about that now is there? You can't change what has happened.'

The words struck Tegan as though she'd been hit.

'You can't change what's happened,' she thought. 'Why didn't I think of it before? Nanna can't change what's happened. But maybe, just maybe, I can. Maybe I can do something to help Alice?'

CHAPTER 5

The War Museum

Tegan sat with a vast plate of burger and chips in front of her. Her eyes were cast on the huge screens on the walls showing clips from films. But her mind was elsewhere. She was thinking about Chrissie and Alice. The conversation about the war had stopped when the waitress had shown them to their table and Tegan didn't know how to get it back on track. After a few moments' silence she decided that the only way was to ask outright.

'What was the date when Alice died?' she asked.

Nanna took a few seconds to register what Tegan was saying.

'Why do you want to know that?' she asked.

Tegan had no ready answer. 'I just do,' she said lamely.

'It was the 6th of January, 1945,' said Nanna, the film clips now forgotten and her eyes looking into the distance, as though she was remembering something. 'In the evening, at about five o'clock,' she added after a few moments' pause. Then the waiter came with their drinks.

Tegan slipped a pen out of her rucksack, grabbed a Hollywood Galaxy Cafe napkin and quickly scrawled '6 Jan' on it, before stuffing it into her pocket. It was a date she knew she must not forget. But she couldn't help thinking that it might already be too late by the next time she made it back. 'After all, who knows what the rules of time are?' she mused.

At least she had done all she could in the meantime. Now what she needed to know was a bit more about daily life back then, so that she wouldn't make too many blunders when she was talking to Chrissie and Alice.

'I wish you'd tell me a bit more about the war,' said Tegan, as innocently as possible. 'Mum can't tell me much as she wasn't even born. I'd like to hear about it.'

'In that case,' said Nanna, looking at her watch. 'What do you say to you and I paying a visit to the Imperial War Museum this afternoon? We've got enough time.'

'Great,' said Tegan. A trip to the Imperial War Museum would be far more exciting even than Hollywood Galaxy Cafe under the present circumstances.

The museum was very busy because of the holidays but Tegan knew exactly where she wanted to go – the 'Home Front' exhibition, which would show her just what life was like for families and children in wartime Britain.

'We had a radio like that,' said Nanna, pointing to a huge shiny brown thing. 'My dad used to listen to Churchill telling us how the war was going. Alice and I always had to keep quiet or we'd get a real telling-off.'

'Was your dad strict?' asked Tegan, getting slightly worried because she hadn't met Chrissie's dad yet!

'No, not really. He wasn't at home much, he always seemed to be on Fire Watch. People had to put out fires that had been started by the bombs.'

After a couple of hours Tegan felt she knew as much as she could before actually going back for herself. They finished the afternoon off with a visit to the museum gift shop. There Tegan spent her pocket money (which she'd brought to London with the intention of buying a present for the new baby) on her own 'Home Front Document Pack.' It had lots of useful information in it. But more importantly it contained documents that looked just like the ones people actually had in wartime. There was a Ration Book and an Identity Card. By this time Tegan knew that everybody had an Identity Card in wartime. It said who you were and where you lived. Now Tegan had one, too. She could fill it in when she got back to Nanna's and take it back with her when she next went to visit Chrissie. Then everyone would believe that she was just another girl living through the war years in London.

Tegan was tired by the time they got back to Nanna's. Not only had it been a long day, but it had been a very eventful one. As Nanna opened the door, Tegan saw the small red, flashing light of the answer machine.

Nanna switched it on and Tegan heard her father's voice. 'Hi, Christine. Hi, Tegan. I hope you're off having fun. I'm just calling to say Mum sends her love and lots of hugs and so do I. Everything's fine here and I'll call you again tomorrow. We miss you . . .'

There was a beep and a click and the machine started to rewind.

'It won't be long before you're home,' said Nanna, putting her arm around Tegan's shoulders.

'No,' said Tegan. 'Not long . . .' and her voice trailed off as she thought just how little time she had to save Alice. There were five days before she was due to go back home. Was that going to be long enough? She didn't even know *when* she'd turn up in the past, or how much time would have gone by between each trip.

'Still,' she thought, 'there's only one way to find out!'

Tegan lay in bed but she just couldn't get to sleep, even though she couldn't remember feeling so tired in ages. She heard Nanna pottering around downstairs. Then she heard her running the taps in the bathroom, before finally hearing the click of a light switch. Nanna had gone to bed.

As quietly as she could, Tegan pulled back the covers and slipped downstairs to the kitchen.

Once safely on the ground floor she switched on the light. She went over to the bowl of fruit on the kitchen table and took two bananas. She then went to the cupboard where she knew Nanna kept the biscuit barrel and took out five chocolate biscuits. Then she quickly switched out the light and crept back upstairs. In her bedroom, she opened her little rucksack and put the fruit and biscuits inside. Tomorrow she would take them with her. From what she had seen at the museum that afternoon, there wasn't much to recommend the food in wartime. And Tegan thought that Chrissie and Alice might just enjoy their new friend dropping by with a treat!

CHAPTER 6

No bananas

Tegan checked the time on her watch and then pulled at the adjustable straps on her rucksack, making sure that it was firmly in place on her back. She wanted to be sure that it made it back with her to the war. It had been mid-afternoon before she had managed to get into the shed. She and Nanna had been shopping on the High Road and then they'd had lunch. It was three o'clock before Nanna went upstairs to do the vacuuming and Tegan had said she'd go into the garden for a breath of fresh air.

Carefully, Tegan pulled the rubber mask over

her face once more and she felt a huge wave of relief as the bunk-beds came in to view. It had worked. The door to the past was still open and if it opened now there was no reason to believe it wouldn't always open.

Tegan lost no time in getting out of the shelter. Now she had work to do. She had to find out what the date was and how much time she had left. Tegan put her hand into her pocket and pulled out the crumpled Hollywood Galaxy Cafe napkin.

'6 Jan,' she read. Tegan shuddered to think that it might already be too late. It had only been a day of her time, but how quickly had time travelled in the past when she wasn't there?

Tegan shuddered again and realized it was because she was cold as well as nervous. As she opened the shelter door, she saw why. Outside lay a thick blanket of snow.

Tegan made her way up the steps with chattering teeth. A few minutes ago she had left a beautiful, sunny spring day and she only had her jeans and a T-shirt on. It had never entered her head that she might need a coat. The snow crunched beneath her trainers as she picked her way along the garden wall. The house still looked the same, thank goodness! She was still in time, she had still beaten the bomb.

Knowing what to expect this time, Tegan knocked on the back door with confidence. It was Chrissie's mother who opened it and she bustled Tegan inside. 'For heaven's sake! What on earth are you doing out there without a coat?' she said, the stern edge in her voice coming more from concern for Tegan than from anger.

'I lost it,' said Tegan. Then thinking very quickly she added, 'And we didn't have enough clothing coupons for a new one.'

Tegan knew by now that even clothes were rationed in wartime and unless you had enough special coupons you couldn't buy new ones.

'Well, come and warm yourself up,' said Chrissie's mum, leading her to the kitchen table. 'You do wear some strange clothes, Tegan. They're American too, I suppose?'

Tegan smiled, but made no response.

'I'm just doing eggs for Chrissie and Alice's

tea,' she continued. 'I dare say we can stretch to some for you, too.'

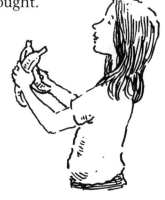

Tegan was excited by the thought of tasting her first real wartime meal. At the same time she knew that it was being very selfish to accept. Food was so scarce and Tegan could eat all she wanted back at Nanna's. Then she remembered the bananas and biscuits she had in her rucksack. 'Maybe they will make up for the eggs,' she thought.

Alice and Chrissie came through into the kitchen, lured by the sound of voices, just as Tegan reached into her rucksack and pulled out the bananas. There were gasps all round.

For a second Tegan thought she had done something terribly wrong, as Chrissie's mum shrieked, 'Where on earth did you get those?' Then she lifted the two bananas up to her face, smelling them and staring at them as though they were diamonds.

Tegan thought it was time for another excuse, and quick! 'My father got them. He said I could bring them. We sometimes get treats at the base,' she added, hoping that it didn't sound too unbelievable.

'I haven't seen a banana in years. I thought there wasn't one to be had in the whole of London and here I am with two in my hands.'

Chrissie's mother smiled at Tegan. 'I don't know,' she said, 'you walk around in weather like this without a coat, but you can get hold of bananas! You're a funny girl.'

Tegan laughed. She was glad that she'd made them so happy with something that seemed so ordinary to her. 'I've got chocolate biscuits, too,' she added hesitantly, not sure if she could handle a reaction like the last one. She was running out of excuses.

Chrissie's mum put the bananas back on the table and the delight on her face changed into a serious expression. 'It's wonderful of you to bring these things for us, Tegan. I really can't believe my eyes, but we just can't accept them. They're far too precious.'

'No, no, they're not,' pleaded Tegan. 'Honestly. I wouldn't have brought them if it wasn't OK.'

She was about to make up another huge lie to try and get herself out of the situation when Chrissie said, 'What's this?'

Tegan turned and saw to her horror that Chrissie had picked up her London Underground Travelcard, complete with a photograph and date stamped '17 April 2001'.

'It must have fallen from my rucksack as I took out the bananas,' she thought.

In a flash, Tegan snatched it from Chrissie's hands. 'Sorry,' she said, realizing how rude she must look. 'Only you shouldn't see that. I need it . . .' Her mind raced. 'I need it to get in and out of the American base.' Tegan thought how easily she was beginning to make up lies when she had to! 'Why didn't I leave it at Nanna's?' she thought. 'Well, I've learnt lesson number two. Leave anything at Nanna's which could give me away!'

'Why did it say 2001?' asked Chrissie.

'It's just a number,' said Tegan. 'My number. We all have numbers.' Chrissie seemed satisfied with the answer.

'I'm hungry,' said Alice.

Tegan let out a large, but silent sigh of relief. 'Good old Alice,' she thought. 'Changing the conversation just when I need it.'

'Me too,' said Chrissie.

'It won't be long,' said Chrissie's mother. Tegan watched closely as she mixed something from a tin with tap water and then took it over to the cooker. 'I'm sure she said she was doing eggs,' thought Tegan. A few seconds later Tegan realized what it was – powdered eggs! She had read about that at the museum. It was dried egg powder that came in tins and didn't really taste like eggs at all. Tegan eagerly awaited a taste, forgetting for a few moments what she had really come for and enjoying all her new experiences.

It was half way through her plateful, which she thought actually tasted rather nice, that Tegan remembered her mission to find out what the date was. She looked around, hoping to see a newspaper lying about or a calendar on the wall. But there was no sign of either. Then Chrissie's mother asked, 'Has that warmed you up?'

'Yes, thank you very much,' replied Tegan.

'Well, why don't you all go through to the sitting-room and let me clear up, ready for when Chrissie's dad gets home. Keep an eye on the clock though, Tegan. It'll be dark before you know it.'

Tegan followed Chrissie and Alice through to

the lounge. It was the first room which she had seen that still looked similar to the one she knew in the present. Its familiarity took Tegan by surprise. It was so easy to forget that this was Nanna's house and that Chrissie was in fact Nanna!

Like the kitchen, the room had tape on the windows and seemed very dark. There was a large horse-hair sofa with little embroidered squares of material hanging over the back. And Tegan noticed a large brown radio sitting on a sideboard. 'That must be the one Nanna was telling me about,' she thought.

Then her eyes caught sight of a tiny wooden stand on the mantel shelf filled with small white cards with numbers printed on them. It was a calendar! 'You must have to change the card by hand every day,' she thought. Silently she made a note of the date. 'December 17,' she read. 'It must be 1944,' she thought. 'Because the war will be over by this time next year.' Tegan counted quickly on her fingers. 'That means it's exactly three weeks until the night of the bomb. And I've only got four days left at Nanna's!'

CHAPTER 7

Working things out

Tegan took a gamble. There had been no snow on the ground last time she'd visited, so maybe more time had passed than she thought.

'How long is it since I was last here?' enquired Tegan, realizing that this was the key to finding out how fast time in the past was travelling.

To her it had only been a day. So had it been a day for them too?

'Don't you know?' asked Chrissie, looking at her as though she might be mad.

'You brought us sweets last week,' said Alice.

Now that Tegan knew several days had passed

she could begin to bluff her way through. 'I know it was last week. I just couldn't remember which day,' she said.

Chrissie thought hard for a few seconds,

'Umm . . . it's just a week ago. Because Dad was out all night on Fire Watch, putting out fires from those bloomin' bombs. Didn't you hear them? It was far worse than usual.'

'Yes, it was, wasn't it,' said Tegan, her confidence slipping. How could Chrissie talk so casually about bombs falling only streets away? For the first time she stopped to think how brave Chrissie and Alice were, keeping calm through all of this. They'd seen things that Tegan couldn't imagine. That she didn't want to imagine.

It also made her realize that while she was here she was also at real risk. She hadn't thought about that before. She was actually in a war zone and if she was to save Alice, then she would have to get caught up in at least one raid herself. This wasn't a game anymore. It wasn't just about playing at living in wartime. This could be life or death. Not only for Alice, but also possibly for herself.

Tegan thought back to the Imperial War Museum. She'd gone in a thing called 'The Blitz Experience'. It was an interactive exhibition where you sat in a large brick shelter and listened to a man pretend there was a raid on. Then you walked out into this bombed-out street they had made look real. Fake smoke had been squirted at them and flickering lights behind windows made it look like there was a fire raging inside. Tegan had thought it was exciting at the time. Now a shiver ran through her at the thought of experiencing it for real. She didn't know if she was ready to cope. But she did know she couldn't leave Alice without trying.

Chrissie broke her thoughts. 'Why weren't you evacuated?' she asked. Tegan smiled to herself. She must remember to give Nanna a hard time when she got back, as payment for all these awkward questions.

'Why weren't you?' she countered, thinking that if they had gone to the country, then Alice would probably have survived.

'I was,' said Chrissie. 'I went to Shropshire, but I hated it. I missed Mum and Alice. Alice was

64

only a tiny baby then, so she stayed with Mum.' Chrissie paused for a second. 'Mrs Hopwell. Bleugh!' she said, pulling a face. 'Mrs Hopwell didn't want to take me. I think they made her. She wanted me to do her housework for her. I got so upset I started to wet the bed and that just made her even meaner. Mum came and saw how unhappy I was and she took me home. I wouldn't go away again after that. Besides, we're winning now, aren't we? Dad says it won't be long before it's all over.'

Tegan wanted to tell them that the war wasn't over yet and that she and Alice would be better off with Mrs Hopwell no matter how mean she was. But it was too late for that now. Now it was up to Tegan.

'So what about you?' Chrissie asked again.

'I . . .' Tegan faltered.

'Tegan, look at the time!' It was Chrissie's mother coming into the room and rescuing her right on cue. 'For goodness sake, you'll be stuck here if you don't get a move on. It won't be long before the blackout goes up. Your mother will be worried sick.'

Tegan quickly got to her feet. She knew it didn't really matter if she got a move on or not, she only had to find her way up the garden. And it had been so interesting listening to Chrissie talk about being evacuated.

'I'll come and see you soon,' she said to Chrissie.

'Yeah,' said Chrissie. 'Or maybe I can come and see you on that American base of yours.'

'You can't, Chrissie,' said Tegan, trying to let her friend down gently. 'Nobody can visit me where I live.' And for the first time she didn't feel as though she was telling a lie.

Tegan trudged back up the garden. 'Next time,' she thought, 'I'll bring my coat and I'll also try to wear something that won't make Chrissie's mum look at me as though I'm an alien!' It was hard trying to come up with explanations and she knew she was bound to make a mistake soon. But it was worth it. Especially for the look on her great-grandmother's face when she'd seen those bananas!

Tegan was halfway up the garden when she

heard a whining sound. It was loud and it was getting louder. For a second or two she stopped to listen. Then she realized what it was. She'd heard it at the museum. It was the unmistakable sound of an air-raid siren.

Tegan fled up the garden, snow and her goosebumps forgotten. She felt like she was in one of those dreams where you keep on running but you don't seem to be getting anywhere and your legs won't work properly. Her trainers slipped on the frozen ground and she had to put out her hands to save herself from falling.

Then she heard the sound of the back door to Chrissie's house opening and muffled voices were carried up the garden on the night air. Tegan realized with mounting horror that they would be hot on her heels to get into the shelter, too. She had to beat them to it. She had to get back to the future before they got there. Or who knew what might happen?

CHAPTER 8

Bridie's house

Tegan half fell down the steps and then flew through the door to the shelter, slamming it behind her. She leaned with her back against it.

'Thank goodness,' she thought as she caught her breath. She could hear the sound of her breathing coming from inside the rubber gas mask once again and, without waiting a second longer, she ripped it from her face. The garden shed appeared before her and she sank on to the bag of peat.

Tegan sat there for several minutes, shaking. Already it seemed so unreal now she was back in the shed. She heard birds singing through the rusty metal roof and opened the door to let some light in. Outside it was a beautiful spring day, the sun was out and there was not a hint of snow to be seen. Tegan remained in the shed for a while, thinking. She had some serious sums to do. It seemed from what Chrissie had said, that a day in Tegan's time was equal to a week in the past. 'Today is Tuesday,' thought Tegan. 'And I go home on Saturday. I've got three more full days. In the past, it's three weeks until the night of the bomb. So if I go back every day, then Friday should be the big day!'

Tegan thought this over again. There was no guarantee things would be the same next time. Maybe she should go straight back now and try to speed things up. Another week might have passed already. She still held the gas mask in her hands and in a second or two she could be back. But no. 'Better leave it as planned,' she thought. 'And not risk messing up what I've managed to sort out so far.'

Tegan wandered back down the garden. She could see Nanna in the kitchen window and waved as she drew closer.

'How long have I been gone this time?' she wondered. Tegan glanced at her watch. It was quarter-past three. She'd been gone no more than fifteen minutes. 'How strange!' she thought. She felt as though she had been gone for hours. 'But I suppose it fits. If a day equals a week, then it makes sense that time is travelling faster in the past,' she mused.

'I was just about to come and find you,' said Nanna as Tegan walked into the kitchen. Tegan's stomach flip-flopped at the thought! 'I usually pop round to Bridie's on a Tuesday,' Nanna continued, 'and take her a few bits of shopping. She can't get out much. Do you mind coming with me?'

Tegan could think of plenty of things she would rather do, but she didn't have much choice. 'Besides,' she thought, 'we did lots of things I wanted to do yesterday.'

'I don't mind,' she said. And then she remembered the conversation she'd had with Chrissie not half an hour ago. 'If you'll tell me more about you and Alice on the way.' With a smile she added, 'Were you ever evacuated?'

* * *

It turned out that Bridie's house was quite close. Nanna rang the bell and when the door

eventually opened, Tegan saw a woman much older than Nanna standing there. She wasn't stooped and frail as Tegan had been expecting. She was actually quite tall for an old person and she still had thick silver-grey hair and sharp eyes. But she did have a cane to help her walk and she was obviously very slow on her feet.

They were welcomed inside and then Tegan sat politely in the lounge answering Bridie's questions about Devon and school and the baby, while Nanna made a cup of tea. 'Tegan's interested in history at the moment,' said Nanna to Bridie. 'I told her about Alice and now she wants to know all about the war.' Nanna turned to Tegan, handing her a mug. 'You should ask Bridie about it. She'll remember more than I can.'

Tegan was taken aback by the mention of Alice. 'How come Bridie knows about her?' she thought.

'Did you know Alice, too?' she asked.

'I knew all of them,' said Bridie with a smile. 'My dad was the local butcher. He had a little shop called O'Neil's, just off the High Road. Your Nanna and her mother used to queue up for their meat rations. And if there was something a bit special coming in, I'd save them a bit or take it round. That's what was called buying things "under the counter".'

Tegan nibbled on a biscuit and listened. At any other time she would probably have found it boring. But now, of course, she hung on to Bridie's every word.

As they walked home an hour or so later

Tegan asked,

'How old is Bridie?'

'Mmm . . . , she must be in her eighties by now,' said Nanna trying to work it out. 'She seemed very grown-up and sophisticated to me during the war. I can remember her wearing gravy browning on her legs to make it look like she had stockings on.'

'Ughh!' said Tegan, wrinkling up her nose. Nanna laughed.

'You didn't want to get caught out in the rain or you ended up with streaky legs!' Nanna said. Tegan giggled and caught Nanna's eye.

'I think Bridie enjoyed this afternoon you know,' said Nanna. 'She likes having someone to share all her memories with.'

'I enjoyed it, too,' said Tegan. And she wasn't just being polite.

* * *

Tegan sat on the sofa watching television. She let her mind wander over her plans for tomorrow. She'd get to the shelter as early as she could.

She'd already sorted out her warmest clothes. Tegan thought about the snow. What would the date be tomorrow when she went back? A week on from the 17th of December. Again Tegan started counting on her fingers and mouthing the dates under her breath, 'Twenty-second, twenty-third, twenty-fourth . . . *twenty-fourth!*' Tegan stopped, her fingers in mid-air. It would be Christmas Eve.

Tegan's mounting excitement mixed with something else that she couldn't quite identify. It would be so amazing to be there on Christmas Eve, but she had an uneasy feeling, too. What was it? Tegan eventually realized what was wrong. When she had been there, there had been no sign of Christmas and yet it had only been a week away. There had been no tree up, no cards on the mantle shelf, no talk of food or presents. Tomorrow, Tegan decided, she would have to go shopping before her trip back. She couldn't afford much, but she had to get Chrissie and Alice something for Christmas.

CHAPTER 9

No ordinary snowball fight

Tegan cast her eyes over the counter of sweets in the newsagents. She had asked Nanna if she could spend some pocket money. As the shop was only on the corner of her street, Nanna had let her go on her own. Tegan tried to decide what to get. She wanted something special for Chrissie and Alice, but she also wanted something that wouldn't arouse too much suspicion. She was beginning to understand what would fit in during wartime and what wouldn't and she didn't want them asking more awkward questions than were strictly necessary!

Tegan settled on a large slab of fruit and nut chocolate and a bag of boiled sweets. She also bought some red crepe paper as part of her Christmas surprise plan.

When she got back to Nanna's, Tegan took everything straight up to her room. She unwrapped the chocolate and broke it into two equal pieces. Then she counted out the sweets until she had two equal piles. There was one left over which Tegan guiltily popped into her mouth. Then she wrapped everything in the red paper until she had four small parcels. Finally, she put them all into her rucksack.

Next came her clothes. Tegan had one skirt with her, which she now put on. Chrissie and Alice didn't seem to wear trousers, even though she knew that lots of women had started to wear them in wartime. Then she pulled on her T-shirt and the only jumper she had with her over the top. It didn't look very 1940s as it was a sweatshirt, but it would have to do. 'It's better than just a T-shirt anyway,' she thought.

Next came her best shoes, which were black patent leather. Tegan thought they looked very suitable. And finally her anorak, which had 'Adidas' written on it, but at least she would be warm. She looked at her reflection in the mirror and thought how she would never normally wear this higgledy-piggledy mixture of clothes. It was warm and sunny again outside. What was Nanna going to think when she came downstairs looking like the abominable snowman? But she was lucky. Halfway down the stairs she heard the phone ring and Nanna came into the hall to answer it.

'I'm just going out in the garden. I won't be long,' Tegan said in an exaggerated whisper to Nanna, who was now trying to concentrate on two conversations at once. Tegan slipped past her and into the kitchen. The fruit bowl had been restocked since she'd taken the bananas and there were now several gleaming oranges sitting in it. Tegan couldn't resist them, however many awkward questions it would mean both from the past and the present. She popped two into her bag.

'Anyway,' she thought, 'it will still be Nanna eating them, just fifty-six years before she'd expected to!' Tegan laughed to herself.

* * *

Five minutes later, with everything in her rucksack that could give her away left in the shed and the time checked on her watch, Tegan found herself once again standing in the snow-covered garden of the past. 'It seems to be so easy and normal, this going backwards and forwards,' she thought.

Tegan heard shouts and squeals floating up to her from further down the garden. A few paces on and she had a clear view. A grin broke across her face. Chrissie and Alice were in the middle of a snowball fight. She was about to shout out to them when she changed her mind, bent down and scooped up a handful of snow. For a few moments she ran unseen before launching her snowball squarely into the middle of Chrissie's back. Chrissie squealed and turned, thinking that it was Alice. Then she saw Tegan.

'You wait!' she shouted, then immediately grabbed at the snow with both hands to launch her revenge attack. Alice joined in and soon Tegan was covered in white splodges and soaked. Snow was everywhere, in her hair and shoes, but it was far too much fun to stop.

Then Chrissie made an enormous snowball.

'This is coming your way and there's no escape,' she panted and threw it as hard as she could. Tegan ducked and it sailed over her head. She stood up laughing at Chrissie for missing her, but noticed that Chrissie had a shocked expression on her face and was looking at something beyond her. Tegan turned round and saw a woman standing behind her with a snowball mark smack-bang in the middle of her coat.

'Chrissie Wilkinson!' shouted the woman, who had obviously just arrived. Tegan's face dropped. Now they were really in trouble. But just when she thought that the woman was about to give them a telling-off, her face broke into a smile. Quick as lightning, she bent down, made a snowball and hurled it in Chrissie's direction. It was all that was needed to get the snowball fight under way once more.

Everyone let Alice hit them at least once, because she was little and not a very good aim. And the woman who had joined in, and who Chrissie and Alice obviously knew, started a two against two fight, taking Alice for her side. The shrieks and laughter escalated until Chrissie's mother opened the back door to see who was making so much noise.

'Have I got half the street ruining my back

garden?' she called, but she didn't seem too upset. The fight calmed down and they all stood rosy-cheeked and exhausted in the rough snow.

'If this war had been fought with snowballs, Hitler would have surrendered long ago if this lot had been let at him,' said the woman to Chrissie's mother, laughing.

Tegan felt a bit shy and looked down at the ground.

'Hello, Tegan, come in and get yourself dry,' said Chrissie's mother, before adding, 'And you, Bridie O'Neil, should know better than to encourage them.'

Bridie! This was Bridie? Tegan couldn't believe it. This pretty young woman who had been running around with them was the same Bridie who now couldn't even make it to the shops alone.

Tegan was shocked. She'd got used to the fact that Chrissie was Nanna and that seemed different somehow. She couldn't quite explain why, but Nanna was just, well, Nanna, and Chrissie was a girl. They were like two different people. Of course, Nanna had grown up or

Tegan wouldn't have been born. But Bridie was an adult in both places, and in the place that Tegan had come from she was an old woman, the kind you saw every day and didn't really think had ever been young. That made it feel weird.

Tegan realized that she was staring and hurried towards the door.

Once inside, Chrissie's mum put the kettle on and made them all take their wet things off. Bridie removed a paper parcel from her pocket. 'Da-dah!' she said with a flourish, putting it on the kitchen table.

'Oh, Bridie!' said Chrissie's mum, 'You managed to get some then?'

Tegan knew that there must be meat in the parcel.

'It's a nice piece of Christmas ham to boil. But listen, a friend of my dad's is saving me two geese over at his shop on the Old Brompton Road. Don't ask me where he got them from, but I'm on my way to pick them up now. One for you, one for me.'

'Bridie, you've just made our Christmas. I

don't know how to thank you,' said Chrissie's mum, clasping the tea caddie to her chest in glee.

'Think nothing of it. All in a day's work,' said Bridie, winking at Tegan. 'Now I'd best be off, before he goes and sells them to someone else. Does anyone want to come with me?'

Chrissie and Alice both let out a deafening, 'Yes,' but Chrissie's mother took control.

'Now, you two, Bridie doesn't want you under her feet. Besides, you've been yawning your head off all morning,' she said to Alice. Turning to Bridie she said, 'I just can't get her to settle down in that shelter.'

'Well, can *I* go?' pleaded Chrissie.

'I don't mind,' said Bridie.

'And what about Tegan?' said Chrissie's mum, looking at Chrissie. Tegan had remained silent throughout, studying Bridie at every opportunity.

'She can come, too,' said Chrissie.

At the thought of a trip into the streets of London, Tegan suddenly found her voice.

'I'd love to,' said Tegan.

'That's settled then,' said Bridie, slapping her hands on her knees and standing up. 'Come on then, let's go.'

Tegan followed Bridie and Chrissie out through the back door.

'This time,' she thought with excitement, 'I'm not going back to the shelter, I'm going on an adventure.'

CHAPTER 10

London at war

Walking around to the front of the house, Tegan saw the street for the first time. The houses looked pretty much as she knew them, only older, which was strange because they were really newer. Tegan realized that it must be because they looked shabby.

'I suppose people don't have time to paint their front door in the middle of a war!' she thought.

Tegan walked with Chrissie and Bridie up to the bus stop on the High Road. It was a walk she knew well, having done it with Nanna several times now and she amused herself by noticing all the differences. Every window was taped with a cross. Sandbags were piled up outside some of the shops and all of them had old shop signs above their doors. There were a few people out and about, children too, and Tegan realized that

her outfit must still look very strange. The girls were wearing thick felt coats with collars and knee-high socks. And the boys were in knee-length shorts. 'Shorts! In this weather?' Tegan thought. She'd like to see the boys at her school wearing those! The bus arrived. It was still a red London bus, very similar to the one she had gone into town on yesterday. Tegan sat down beside Chrissie.

'I don't have any money for the fare,' she whispered, suddenly scared that she'd be thrown off and never find her way back to the house.

'Don't worry,' Chrissie whispered back. 'Bridie will pay.'

Tegan settled back in her seat to watch the world go by. She felt as if she was on some kind of strange theme-park ride. This ride would be called 'Travel Through Wartime London,' Tegan thought and smiled to herself. This was more exciting than any theme park!

'What are you doing tomorrow?' Tegan asked Chrissie.

'We always go to church on Christmas morning,' said Chrissie. 'And we'll have a big dinner. Mum's been saving rations for weeks.'

'Will you get presents?' asked Tegan.

'Well, I'm hanging up my stocking, that's for sure.'

Tegan sat holding on to her rucksack full of

goodies, pleased that she would be able to leave them a small surprise for when they woke up tomorrow.

'Come on, girls. Look lively, it's our stop,' said Bridie jumping up.

Bridie had a quick chat with the butcher at the back of his shop and in no time the three of them were walking back out on to the busy street. Bridie had one goose, wrapped up, under her arm and had given the other to Chrissie and Tegan to manage between them.

'I can't face another journey as slow as the one coming. Let's go back on the tube,' said Bridie.

Tegan was disappointed. She liked going by bus because she could stare out of the window. The Underground would look just the same as it did in the present. 'A tunnel's a tunnel after all, no matter what year it is,' she thought.

At Earls Court tube station, Bridie paid for their tickets and Chrissie and Tegan started to take the steps down to the platform. Tegan felt she could almost be back in the present. It all looked so familiar, even down to the red, circular station sign. But she was in for a shock when she turned to walk on to the platform.

The platform was packed. But not only with people waiting to get the train, but with people who looked as if they were living down there. There were whole families with babies and children, sitting on blankets with their suitcases by their side. Some people were even lying down, trying to get some sleep. One family was trying to prepare some kind of a picnic. Tegan noticed they had to keep lifting up their plates to stop people treading on them as they passed by. Tegan had heard that the Underground stations had been used as shelters, but she hadn't been expecting this!

'Go up to the end, Chrissie,' said Bridie, with a guiding hand on her back. 'There might be a bit more room.'

Tegan followed Chrissie, carefully picking her way amongst people and their belongings. 'What a horrible way to spend Christmas Eve,' she thought. They would have a long wait until Christmas morning when it would be safe enough to go back to their homes.

As they drew nearer the end of the platform, Tegan thought she could hear music. Then she began to make out the words of 'Good King Wenceslas'. At least a dozen people were sitting together singing, tin mugs in their hands and luggage at their side. Tegan noticed they had tried to make it look a bit Christmassy and had strung a coloured paper-chain around themselves. It looked very cosy and everyone seemed to be having a great time.

Bridie stopped where the platform ran out and one of the men in the group caught her eye. 'Won't you join us in a carol?' he asked, getting up to make way for them to join the group. Chrissie and Tegan found themselves coaxed into the circle.

'Well, just the one then,' said Bridie. 'After all, it is Christmas.'

Tegan looked at the scene around her with wide eyes and joined in with the chorus of 'O, Come All Ye Faithful', smiling at Chrissie as they belted the words out.

The train pulled in alongside the platform as they finished the last verse. Saying their

goodbyes, Tegan thought how she'd been wrong to think everyone down here would have a horrible Christmas. They were making the best of it and having fun. In fact, Tegan thought, they seemed to be having much more fun than a lot of people she knew in the present.

Back at the house Tegan watched Chrissie and Alice hang their stockings from the fireplace. She was glad they'd done it early because now she might be able to pop the presents in herself, rather than give them to Chrissie's mum and have to come up with yet more explanations.

Tegan chose her moment carefully and when the girls were called into the kitchen to help carry the tea through, she jumped up from the sofa, pulled open her rucksack and with her hands full of red-paper parcels and oranges, quickly stuffed them into the toes of the stockings. She made it in the nick of time and flung herself back on the sofa, trying to keep the smile from her face. How surprised and delighted everyone would be when Chrissie and Alice emptied their stockings the next morning! Tegan wished she could be there to see it. But that was impossible.

She had to keep on track because she would soon have a far more important mission to deal with. Besides, they'd expect her to be having Christmas at the American base. Tegan cast her mind back to the tube station. 'I've already had my taste of Christmas,' she thought. 'And it was far more special than I could ever have imagined.'

CHAPTER 11

Dangerous questions

'Merry Christmas, Tegan,' said Chrissie as Tegan stood at the back door.

'Merry Christmas, Chrissie,' Tegan replied. Then she turned to Alice, who, as always, was holding Monkey. 'I hope Father Christmas brings you something special,' she said.

'Me too,' smiled Alice. 'And Monkey says Happy Christmas, too.'

Tegan left, making sure that no one watched her walk back up the garden. She'd had such a great afternoon. For the first time as she approached the shelter she really didn't want to leave. Tegan stood in the doorway, hesitating. For a split second the thought crossed her mind to stay in the past. But then she realized that unless she was there on that important day, the 6th of January, it would soon be a very different family. It would be a family without Alice. She had to keep to her plan.

Tegan pulled open the shelter door and went inside. She took the mask from her face and the garden shed reappeared once again.

* * *

'That was Bridie on the phone,' said Nanna as Tegan walked into the kitchen. Tegan looked at her watch. 'Surely I must have been gone more than a few minutes this time?' she thought. Her watch told her that she had been gone about half an hour.

'She's got some jumble that she wants me to pick up for the Easter Fair,' continued Nanna. 'I know we only went there yesterday, but . . .'

'I don't mind,' said Tegan, who was thrilled at the thought of seeing Bridie again. Then she ran upstairs to change before Nanna had a chance to ask her about her strange outfit.

* * *

Tegan stared at Bridie just as much now as she had done on first meeting her in the past. This time she noticed the similarities, the things that had stayed with Bridie through all the years in between. There was her smile and the way she laughed with a throaty giggle. 'Those things haven't changed at all,' thought Tegan. Then there was the way she had winked at Tegan when she walked into the room, in just the same way as she'd winked at her in Chrissie's kitchen. That had really made Tegan feel weird. Almost as though Bridie knew who she was, but Tegan knew there was no chance of that.

Then she had an idea. Bridie might not realize that she was the same girl she'd met so many years ago, but would Bridie remember her at all? Would she remember the girl who she'd taken with Chrissie to fetch the Christmas goose in 1944? Tegan desperately wanted to ask her but didn't know if she dare.

That was one area she'd left well alone, the mixing of the past with the present. She had deliberately never asked Nanna if she remembered her American friend, because it would all get too complicated.

What if Nanna started to remember things that hadn't even happened yet? What if she started to tell her about the night Alice was killed and Tegan began to appear in the story herself? Tegan knew that was ridiculous, because if she hadn't been back there on that night yet, then Nanna couldn't possibly remember it. But then again, who knew what happened when you started playing around with time?

Tegan's curiosity finally got the better of her. 'Bridie,' she started cautiously, 'what was Christmas like during the war?'

'Oh, we had some fun. Hitler couldn't stop that,' she replied.

Tegan thought she'd have to try another route. She could be here all day with tales of other wartime Christmases. 'Was there turkey for dinner?'

'We had a goose one year. My father, being a butcher, could get us treats sometimes,' said Bridie. And Tegan knew she had her opening

'Did you get treats for Nanna's family, too?' she asked.

'We did that year. Your Nanna and a friend of hers came with me to collect them I think.'

'What was she like . . . the friend?' asked Tegan, bursting with excitement.

'An American girl if I remember rightly. At least I think that's what Chrissie's mother said.'

Tegan felt the palms of her hands go sweaty and she suddenly felt very hot. Bridie had remembered her. Bridie was proof that this wasn't all a dream.

'What happened to her?' asked Tegan, getting carried away now and wanting to know if there was any more Bridie could remember.

Bridie looked puzzled. 'What happened to her?' she repeated. 'I don't know. I only met her the once, I think. You'll have to ask your grandmother. They seemed as thick as thieves.'

Tegan let out the breath she hadn't realized she had been holding in until that moment.

'Of course,' thought Tegan. 'Bridie can't remember any more because we have only met once in the past. Still, it does mean that this is really happening. I am actually changing history. And if I can do it for Bridie, then I can do it for Alice, too.'

They were back at the house, doing the washing-up together after dinner, when Nanna asked Tegan what she would like to do the following day.

'Oh, not much,' said Tegan, trying to sound casual, but all the time thinking how the most important thing was that she must make her next trip back.

'I'm happy just messing around in the garden,' she added.

'You're easy to please,' said Nanna. 'Don't you want to go out somewhere?'

'Not really,' said Tegan. 'Besides,' she said, thinking of a good excuse. 'We hadn't better go far in case Dad calls. It's only a day or two until Mum has the baby.'

'Yes, you're right,' said Nanna. 'You know,' she said, changing the subject, 'I heard you chatting to Bridie about my little American friend this afternoon.'

Tegan dropped the spoons she was drying with a clatter on the kitchen floor. Nanna carried on talking as Tegan bent to pick them up. 'We had a lot of fun together. But I've been thinking about it all afternoon and I can't for the life of me think where she disappeared to.' Tegan didn't say a word.

'Are you all right, Tegan?' asked Nanna looking concerned. 'You look a bit pale.'

CHAPTER 12

The gift

Tegan lay in bed. The house was silent. All she could hear was the rhythmic ticking of the bedside clock. A shaft of light streamed in through a chink in the curtains. 'Another sunny day,' thought Tegan. She listened for sounds of Nanna clattering about downstairs, but couldn't hear anything. She thought back to their conversation the previous evening. Tegan had been so quiet and pale after Nanna had mentioned her 'American friend' that Nanna had got quite worried. Tegan smiled to herself. 'If only she knew the real reason!' At least it meant that Nanna would be happy for her to stay around the house today, in case she was coming down with something.

Tegan turned over and snuggled deeper into her duvet. 'Only two more trips back,' she thought. She was going to miss them when she went home. Tegan counted on her fingers again. Today's trip would bring her out on December 31st, New Year's Eve. 'That might be fun,' she thought. And tomorrow's would bring her out on the day she had been waiting for, the day she was going to try to change history forever.

Tegan shivered slightly at the thought, despite being in her cosy bed. In a way she wished it was tomorrow, wished she could get it over and done with. But she had to play by the rules she'd been given and that would mean another trip back today. 'So I might as well make the most of it,' she thought. Tegan turned to look at the clock on her bedside table. 'Half-past ten!' she said out loud in surprise, flinging back the bedclothes. 'Why didn't Nanna wake me?'

Walking through the hall a few minutes later, she realized that she still hadn't heard a sound from Nanna. 'Where is she?' Tegan wondered. It was as Tegan walked into the kitchen and looked through the window that she saw exactly where Nanna was. Tegan gasped, momentarily rooted to the spot. Nanna was at the bottom of the garden and she was clearing out the shed!

Tegan didn't lose a second. She flung open the back door and went running up the garden. 'Nanna! Nanna!' she called.

Nanna put down the clay pots she had just brought out on to the grass and smiled at Tegan. 'Hello, sleepyhead,' said Nanna. 'I didn't want to disturb you. How do you feel?'

Tegan scanned the grass. It was covered with things from the shed. Her eyes darted around for her precious box, but she couldn't see it. This was a disaster. Where was the mask? What had Nanna done with it? And how would she ever get back again without it? Not only that, but if Nanna was in the shed, how could Tegan use it today? And Tegan knew that if she didn't get back today then everything would be ruined.

She was finding it hard to fight back tears and stop her voice from shaking. 'Fine thanks. I . . . I didn't realize you were going to do this today,' she eventually managed.

'I wasn't going to. But you were asleep, so it seemed like a good time to get on with some jobs.'

Tegan swallowed hard, not trusting her voice. 'Why did I have to go and oversleep,' she thought. 'This is all my own fault.'

'There's so much junk in here,' said Nanna. 'Half of this stuff can be thrown out.'

'No!' Tegan shouted, not realizing that her voice was going to be quite so powerful. Nanna stopped and looked at her in surprise. 'I mean . . . ,' faltered Tegan, 'that I'd like to have a look through it first, if that's all right.'

Nanna smiled again. 'Of course you can, but I

don't think you'll find much. Come on, give me a hand. You can't see a thing in there it's so dingy. Goodness knows how four of us used to stay down there night after night. There's not enough room to swing a cat!'

Tegan went through the door of the shed. She was glad that it was dark inside because she felt a hot tear spring to the corner of her eye. She quickly wiped it away and swallowed hard again. It didn't look like her shed any more. This was her own secret place, she knew all its shapes and smells. But now it was half-empty and changed. And where was her box? Tegan cast her eyes towards the shelf at the far end, where after each visit to the past she had carefully replaced the mask. The shelf was empty.

'Let's get this bag of peat out,' said Nanna. 'We can manage it between us.'

Tegan bent down and helped Nanna lift the bag, the bag that she had used as a seat and where she had done most of her thinking. All Tegan's plans were unravelling before her eyes. She was even having to help destroy them.

Back outside, Tegan took some deep breaths.

She'd think of something, she had to.

Nanna came up behind her. 'I've got something to show you,' she said. 'Something I think you might be very interested in.'

Tegan turned around to see that Nanna was holding a small box. A box with scrawly writing on the outside that Tegan knew without a second glance read: 'Alice Wilkinson'. She felt her body relax and relief flooded through her. Her box was safe.

'I found this at the back of the shed. It must have been there for years,' said Nanna, handing it to Tegan. 'Open it.'

Tegan didn't need another invitation. She took the box in silence and opened the lid. Nanna watched her carefully. Tegan pulled out the familiar rubber mask, as familiar to her now as any of her own possessions.

'It was Alice's,' said Nanna. 'It's her gas mask. If you'd like it, you can keep it.'

Tegan's face broke into a broad grin. 'Oh, Nanna,' she said, flinging her arms around her grandmother. 'I'd love to. Thank you.'

With her box safely by her side, Tegan worked

as hard as she could to clear out the shed and replace the things being kept. The sooner the job was done, thought Tegan, the sooner she could make her trip. And time was pushing on. As things went back inside, the shed began to look more familiar and Tegan's spirits rose. It had been a close call and not one that she wanted to repeat. But no harm had been done. Before the afternoon was out she would once again be in the past and one step nearer to her goal.

Nanna was pleased to see Tegan's enthusiasm over the mask and even more pleased, if a little puzzled, by her keenness to help with the shed.

'I think Alice would be glad to know you're interested in her,' said Nanna. 'I'm sure she'd be pleased that you are the one looking after her mask.'

'So am I,' said Tegan. Nanna could have no idea just how true her words were.

CHAPTER 13

All Clear

Tegan was exhausted. She sat down on her old bag of peat, dirty, tired, but very happy. The shed wasn't quite the same as before, but as long as it would still take her into the past, Tegan didn't care. She brushed dried mud from the leg of her jeans. There would be no time to change before returning this time. It was already the middle of the afternoon and Nanna thought she was just finishing off the tidying up inside. She would have to get a move on. Tegan took her precious mask out of its box. Now it really was hers. She could keep it forever. She could take it with her to Devon and who knows? When she next came to visit Nanna, she could bring it back with her and see if it still held its magic!

Tegan put it on and the tidy new shed turned into the tidy makeshift home of the shelter. The sight was as common to her eyes now as the shed itself. She noticed that here too somebody had been in it since her last visit. There was a half-drunk mug of tea standing by a Thermos flask and several books that she hadn't seen before. Tegan looked at the cover of one. *Girl's Own Stories*, she read, looking at a picture of two cheery girls in hats and coats, similar to those she had seen children wearing on her trip to the Underground.

Tegan opened the door of the shelter. As she walked up the steps a smell of burning hit her nostrils. The air reminded Tegan of how it smelt on Bonfire Night, strong wood smoke mixed with the cold air. As she walked towards the house Tegan noticed something else. There was a distant haze of smoke rising beyond the rows of houses. Tegan knew then that somewhere, not too far away, a bomb must have landed.

When Chrissie's mother came to the back door, she didn't greet Tegan with her usual warm smile. She looked a little pale and shaken and very surprised to find Tegan on her doorstep.

'How on earth did you get here so quickly?' she asked. 'The "All Clear" only sounded a few minutes ago.'

'I ran,' said Tegan. 'I wanted to make sure you were all OK. That one was pretty close.' Tegan was very proud of herself these days for the way she managed to make up excuses on the spot!

'You can say that again,' said Chrissie's mother, ushering her inside.

Once inside, Tegan found Chrissie and Alice in a state of excitement.

'Can we go and look?' asked Chrissie. 'Please, the "All Clear's" gone. We'll be quite safe.'

'I want to go,' said Alice. 'Monkey will look after me.'

The truth was that Chrissie's mum was anxious to see for herself just what damage had been caused and if she could help out in any way.

'Come on then,' she said, grabbing her coat

from the back of the kitchen door. 'Get your coats on. And for heaven's sake stay close to me. I don't know what we're going to find out there.'

Tegan felt a mixture of fear and excitement run through her veins. She had no idea what to expect.

As they neared the High Road, the smell of burning grew stronger and Tegan could hear the bell of a fire engine. She was thrilled and scared all at the same time. This was it. This was like the 'Blitz Experience' in the museum. But this was for real.

As they turned the corner on to the High Road, Chrissie's mother stopped in her tracks. 'I don't believe it,' she whispered, bringing her hand up to her mouth. They had been walking so fast that Tegan nearly went crashing into her.

Tegan looked up to see what had made her stop so suddenly and her eyes fell on a huge crater. All Tegan could see in front of her was debris. Bricks and wood from demolished shops lay strewn around what had recently been a busy high street. There seemed to be lots of men in tin hats searching amongst the rubble. Tegan thought that they must be looking for people and her stomach turned in knots at the idea.

Then Chrissie's mum turned to the three of them. 'Bridie,' she said. All colour had gone from her face now. 'The butcher's shop!'

The four of them ran as quickly as they could. Tegan stumbled over broken bricks, but didn't fall. Her mind raced. Bridie had to be all right. She *knew* Bridie was alive. They reached the shop, or what was left of it. Half of it was still standing, but Tegan noticed the 'O'Neil's Butchers' sign, broken and lying amongst the rubble. Now it only read 'O'Nei' and was covered in a thick layer of brick dust.

'Bridie!' called Chrissie.

'Bridie,' echoed Alice in her small voice.

Bridie emerged from the chaos. 'I'm here, it's

all right. I'm OK.'

Chrissie and Alice flung themselves at Bridie's skirt. Tegan hesitated and then did the same.

'Look at the shop,' said Chrissie's mum in disbelief.

'I know,' said Bridie. 'But we're all fine. That's the main thing.'

Tegan released her grip and looked over the scene. She saw two men carrying a stretcher from one of the ruined buildings. She looked away quickly. Bridie was right, the shop could be rebuilt. The main thing was that Bridie wasn't hurt.

'Come back with us and have a cup of tea,' said Chrissie's mum.

'I should stay with Dad and sort things out,' said Bridie.

'You can do that after a cup of tea,' said Chrissie's mum firmly and she took Bridie by the hand and led her through the ruins. 'You've had a nasty shock.'

Now that the panic was over, Tegan looked around as they walked back home. She was amazed to see a smartly dressed woman in hat and gloves walk past the scene as though there was nothing wrong at all. She didn't even take a second glance at the huge crater.

'How can people get so used to all this that they don't really see it any more?' Tegan asked Chrissie.

Chrissie shrugged. 'You just do, I suppose. Don't you?' she asked. And Tegan realized that the only reason Chrissie had taken such an interest in this was because it was at the end of her road and not at the end of someone else's.

Tegan looked up at the barrage balloon floating up above them. It was suspended in mid-air and supposed to stop enemy aircraft from flying too low over the city. 'This bomb still got through,' she thought and she knew that another would, too. There was another bomb destined for Chrissie's street and when it came, Tegan would have to be there, too. 'Next time I'll be here when it happens,' she thought and she turned back to wait for Alice, who was trailing behind them.

* * *

'I'll see you next week,' said Tegan to Chrissie as she got up to leave the comfort of Chrissie's sofa. 'Happy New Year.'

'Right now I don't know that we've got much to be happy about!' said Chrissie's mum.

'The war will end in 1945. You'll see,' said Tegan, wishing they would believe what she knew.

'I hope you're right, love, I really do,' came the tired reply.

Tegan left with mixed feelings. Maybe Chrissie's mum was right to feel beaten. After all, Tegan knew what was about to happen to Alice. But Tegan also knew that she was going to do everything in her power to change that.

As she made her way up the garden, Tegan turned around to look at the house. She looked at the barrage balloon floating above and listened to faint noises from the High Road. 'I'll be back tomorrow,' she whispered. 'I'll be back for Alice.'

CHAPTER 14

Family album

Tegan couldn't eat her dinner. Her stomach felt like it did the night before a test at school, especially a maths test.

'Are you sure that you're all right?' said Nanna.

'I'm fine,' said Tegan, pushing baked beans around her plate with a fork, her mind elsewhere.

'Tomorrow,' she thought, 'it will all be over.'

The phone rang and Nanna answered it. It was her dad and Tegan took the receiver.

'Hi, Dad. How's things? How's Mum?'

'She's fine,' came Dad's reassuring voice down the line. 'I was calling to tell you that they're going to induce the baby tomorrow. So by tomorrow night you'll have a little brother or sister.'

Now there were two major events that would have happened by this time tomorrow.

'Induce?' said Tegan. 'What does that mean?'

'It's nothing to worry about,' said Dad. 'It just means that they help the baby along. Lots of babies are born that way. And it also means that I'll be able to come and pick you up on Saturday and bring you home.'

At the mention of the word 'home' Tegan thought how very far away it seemed. It suddenly felt as though she'd been in London for weeks. 'Right now,' Tegan thought, 'I would give anything to be at home with Mum and Dad. For everything to be over.' But she knew that these feelings would pass. Tomorrow when she went into the shed she would be strong and brave, just like Chrissie and Alice were. They would go through it all together.

That night, as she got ready for bed, Tegan

asked Nanna one last time about Alice. She needed to be as prepared as possible. She wanted to know what to expect. When Nanna had been through the story again, Tegan asked her one last question.

'Nanna, do you ever wonder what Alice would be like now if she was alive?'

'Sometimes,' said Nanna. 'It would be nice to have a sister. You know, however much you argue and fall out, brothers and sisters still love each other. You remember that when you get back home.'

'I will,' said Tegan.

* * *

Tegan slept fitfully. Her dreams were all mixed up and she kept waking with feelings of panic. 'You'll be all right,' she kept telling herself. 'Everything will be all right.' But the dreams lasted until morning. In them, it wasn't Alice but the new baby that didn't make it to the shelter. Tegan tried to call out, but realized that she didn't even know the baby's name.

Eventually Tegan woke herself up by calling out loud, 'Come back . . .'

She sat up in bed, taking deep breaths, just as Mum always told her to do when she got worked up about something. Tegan looked around the room and her eyes fell on the dressing table. Sitting on top was her precious box. Ever since Nanna had given it to her, it hadn't left her side. And last night she had brought it into the house rather than leave it in the shed. She went over to the dressing table and sat down in front of the mirror. Tegan opened the box and took out the mask. She turned it over in her hands and then looked up at herself in the mirror.

'You can do it,' she told herself, seriously.

Then she put it back in its box and climbed into bed.

Tegan knew that there was no point in going to the shed too early. From what Nanna had said, the air raid would be at about five o'clock. That would already mean that she would have to make up some excuse to Chrissie and her mum for being there after dark.

'If I get there mid-afternoon, I'll be in plenty of time,' she thought. That meant she had to find a way of passing the time until then. Tegan restlessly moved around the house. She tried to read or watch TV, but she couldn't concentrate.

Nanna noticed that Tegan seemed to be looking for something to do. 'Would you like to look through my old photo album?' she said. 'You might find a picture of Alice in there.'

Tegan's face lit up. 'That'd be great,' she said, wondering why she hadn't thought to ask Nanna if she had any pictures before.

Nanna fetched the album and Tegan said nothing as her grandmother talked about the photos, but she recognized everyone.

There was one of Chrissie in the back garden. Tegan knew that it must have been taken before the war because there were flowers still growing in the garden. It hadn't been covered in vegetables.

There was another, of Alice as a small baby.

'That's the only photograph I've got of her,' said Nanna. 'We didn't take many in wartime.'

Tegan studied the picture carefully and then moved on to look at the others. There were pictures of Chrissie celebrating the end of the war at a street party, greedily stuffing a sandwich into her mouth. There was one of Bridie outside the newly rebuilt butcher's shop. Tegan noticed that they had a new and more modern 'O'Neil's' sign outside. Then Tegan came to one of a young woman sitting on a beach, with two older people in the background.

'That was taken on holiday in Weymouth. I was about twenty, I think,' said Nanna. Tegan carefully lifted the photograph from its mounts to study it more closely. 'Yes,' she thought, you could still tell that it was Chrissie and that it was her parents behind her.

'I think you look very pretty,' said Tegan.

Nanna blushed. 'You can keep it if you'd like,' she said. 'I'll find a little frame.' And Nanna left her looking at the pictures while she went in search of one.

Tegan looked at her watch. She'd been so carried away spotting people and places in the pictures that time really had flown.

Nanna came back into the room holding a small wooden picture frame. She took the photograph from Tegan and fixed it behind the glass.

'There,' she said, looking pleased with herself. 'It fits perfectly.' She handed it to Tegan. 'Now,' she said, 'I'm going to make a cake for when your dad arrives tomorrow. A celebratory birthday cake,' she laughed.

Tegan knew that the time had come. There was no going back. She went upstairs and picked up the box from her dressing table.

'Good luck,' she said to herself in the mirror, before going downstairs and telling Nanna she was just going out into the garden for a while.

CHAPTER 15

Going back

It was a calm, sunny afternoon. Cotton wool clouds bobbed in the sky and a sparrow swooped down on to Nanna's freshly dug garden, looking for worms. 'Tonight,' thought Tegan, 'this will be a different world for me.' A shudder ran down her back and before she had time to lose her nerve she ran into the shed, shutting the door behind her.

Tegan lifted the mask to her face. 'One second, I'm here and in the blink of an eye, I'm there,' she thought. She took a deep breath, as if she were just about to jump into deep water from the side of a swimming pool. Then she put the mask on.

Once she had taken the plunge, her nerves vanished. She felt confident. She was in the shelter. It was 6 January 1945 and she was here to save Alice. Without any hesitation Tegan opened the door on the wartime world.

The day that greeted her came as a surprise. For the first time the sun was shining in a watery, winter way. The garden, which was usually grey and cold, looked almost pretty. Tegan walked down it in purposeful strides and thought how strange it was that the worst things can happen on the nicest of days.

It was Alice who came to the door when she tapped on it. Alice and Monkey. She ran inside to tell Chrissie, shouting, 'It's Tegan!'

When Tegan came in, the big, brown radio was on and Chrissie was still laughing from something she had heard on it.

'Hi, Chrissie,' said Tegan.

'Hello,' said Chrissie. She sat back on the sofa and waited for Tegan to join her. 'You're dead lucky not having any brothers or sisters,' said

Chrissie. Then she pointed towards Alice. 'She just won't shut up when I'm trying to listen.' Alice stuck her tongue out at Chrissie and Chrissie did the same in return. Tegan sat quietly on sofa, thinking about what Nanna had told her last night about brothers and sisters loving each other really.

Tegan's eye caught the little calendar on the mantle shelf. At first she didn't register that anything was wrong and her eyes moved over it. Her brain caught up a few seconds later and she looked back. It read, 'January 5'.

'January 5th,' thought Tegan in panic. 'But it can't be. I can't have come back on the wrong date, I just can't.'

'Chrissie,' she said, so loudly and panic-stricken that Chrissie immediately stopped taunting Alice to look at her. 'What date is it?'

Chrissie hesitated at such a strange question wondering why Tegan was always on about dates and times.

'It's January 6th,' she said.

'The 6th,' repeated Tegan. 'You're sure it's the 6th?'

'Yes. Why?' asked Chrissie, growing impatient with Tegan's strange behaviour.

Tegan pointed to the calendar. 'It . . . it says it's the fifth today.'

Chrissie followed Tegan's arm to look where she was pointing.

'Dad must have forgotten to change it over this morning. I'll do it,' said Chrissie, leaping to her feet. And as Tegan sank back on to the cushion with relief, Chrissie brought the calendar forward until it told her that it was January 6th. The day Tegan had been waiting for.

Time passed slowly. 'It always does when you're waiting for something,' thought Tegan. She watched Alice like a hawk, her eyes following her every move and her stomach lurching whenever Alice went to leave the room without taking Monkey with her. 'It's OK,' said Tegan to herself. 'Nothing will happen until it's dark.'

The afternoon drew on and Tegan knew that she was going to have a problem when darkness fell. Chrissie's mum would want her to get home in daylight, well before the blackout went up and the city was plunged into inky blackness.

As the light began to fade, Tegan decided what she must do.

'Chrissie,' she said, 'will you hide me here?'

'What?' said Chrissie, thinking how strange Tegan had been all afternoon.

'When your mum comes in, will you tell her that I've already gone home and then hide me behind the sofa?'

Alice heard the conversation and thought it sounded like a great game.

'*I* will,' she said eagerly.

'Will you?' repeated Tegan to Chrissie, looking at her earnestly.

'But why?' said Chrissie. 'What on earth for?'

For a second Tegan thought about telling her the truth. But she knew that she couldn't. She couldn't risk anything now. 'Chrissie . . . ,' Tegan started. 'I can't tell you why, but please trust me.' Tegan held Chrissie's gaze. 'There is a good reason, I promise. I wouldn't ask you if there wasn't. I really need your help.'

Chrissie was silent, weighing things up in her

mind. She wondered how much trouble she would get into later when her mother found out. A lot, probably. But Tegan was her friend. A good friend now and if she needed her help, then Chrissie decided she would give it. 'OK,' she said.

Alice cheered and Tegan, not realizing until then just how tense the moment had been, flung her arms around a surprised Chrissie in gratitude.

Minutes later, Chrissie's mum came into the lounge and Tegan slipped behind the sofa in the nick of time.

'Where's Tegan?' she asked.

'She's gone,' said Chrissie. 'She went a while ago. You must have been upstairs.'

'Strange,' said Chrissie's mum. 'I never heard her.' Then she turned her attention to other matters. 'Your dinner will be ready soon. I'll call you when it's on the plates.' And with that she left the room.

Chrissie and Alice both darted around the back of the sofa to see Tegan crouched on her knees.

'That was close,' said Tegan.

'I wish I knew what you were up to,' said Chrissie. 'Are you coming back out?'

'No, I'll stay here,' said Tegan, knowing that she wasn't going to wait much longer, because as she lifted her eyes towards the window, she could see that it was almost dark.

CHAPTER 16

The siren's wail

'How long are you going to stay there?' asked Chrissie. 'You can't spend the night behind our sofa.'

Tegan looked up into Chrissie's worried face. Alice was standing by her side. Tegan noticed immediately that she didn't have Monkey.

'Where's Monkey, Alice?' Tegan asked, ignoring Chrissie's questions.

'He's over there,' said Alice pointing to a spot on the floor which Tegan couldn't see from where she was hiding.

'Go and get him,' snapped Tegan, in a harder

tone than she'd intended. Alice looked hurt.

'Why are you picking on Alice?' Chrissie asked, cross that anyone else would try and speak to Alice in a tone that was reserved for sisters.

'I'm not, I . . . '

But Tegan didn't have time to finish her sentence before a faint wailing sound could be heard in the room. And it made Tegan's heart miss a beat.

The sound grew louder. Tegan froze. She could see herself from the outside, crouched behind the sofa, Chrissie and Alice standing over her. And for a second nobody moved. Then all hell broke loose.

'It's Moaning Minnie. Come on. You'll have to come out now,' said Chrissie. 'We'll have to go down the shelter.'

Tegan sprang to her feet. 'There's no time to lose,' she thought. 'This is it! Keep calm,' she told herself. 'Keep calm . . . Where's Alice? Where's Monkey? Keep calm . . .'

As Tegan collected her thoughts, Chrissie's mum walked into the room. She stopped in her tracks when she saw Tegan. 'What are you . . . ?' she began to ask before trailing off and adding, 'Oh, never mind. We'll sort it out later. Come on, quickly, all of you. Get your coats on and get out.'

Tegan had waited for this moment for so long. She had every move rehearsed in her head. She'd imagined what it would feel like to be in the middle of the raid. But now she was actually here, it didn't feel anything like it. There was so much noise and confusion.

Chrissie and Alice ran out of the room to fetch their coats. Tegan's eyes fell on Monkey, still lying in the middle of the rug. She bent down and picked him up.

'I've done it,' she thought. 'I've got Monkey. That's what matters. He hasn't been forgotten.'

'Tegan,' said Chrissie's mum, rapidly losing her patience. 'For goodness sake, leave that. Come on. We have to get out.'

Her words brought Tegan back to focus on what was happening. She clasped Monkey to her and followed Chrissie and Alice out of the lounge. When Tegan caught up with them, they were standing by the back kitchen door, which was open.

'Dad's gone up with the oil lamp,' said Chrissie.

Alice noticed that Tegan was holding Monkey.

'Monkey!' she exclaimed in delight, holding her arms out to take him.

Tegan handed him over. Everything was going to be OK.

* * *

But outside, everything was far from OK. Tegan looked out into the night. She could hear the ground guns firing at planes in the distance, their yellow flash momentarily lighting up the night sky. The siren continued to moan and wail and, underneath it, Tegan could hear another sound. It had started faintly, but now it was getting louder. It was the drone of a plane's engine and it was heading their way.

'Run!' shouted Chrissie's mum to all three of them, virtually pushing them through the doorway.

'I can't believe they didn't give us more warning,' she muttered under her breath. Chrissie's mother was scared, really scared, but she knew that she couldn't show it.

Tegan took a last glance down at Alice as she headed through the door. Alice had Monkey clenched in her fist.

'It's going to be OK,' Tegan told herself. 'So long as Alice has Monkey, we'll all be safe.' And she headed out into the terrible night.

Tegan ran for her life. Her sights were firmly set on the shelter. Why did it seem so far away all of a sudden? Tegan could feel Alice running at her heels and see Chrissie a couple of paces in front of her. The smell of gun smoke seared into Tegan's nostrils. Great flashes kept lighting up the night sky as bright as day and each was accompanied by the booming sound of gunfire.

Above it all, Tegan could hear her own rasping breath and as she breathed out, clouds of white mist disappeared into the night air behind her. Her foot-falls thudded on the wet ground as the drone of the enemy planes came ever nearer.

'Monkey! I haven't got Monkey,' came a wailing voice through the darkness.

The words made Tegan's blood run cold. She stopped in her tracks and turned to see Alice start heading back towards the house.

This couldn't be happening. Tegan's eyes darted in every direction. What was going on? Where was Monkey? Alice hadn't forgotten him. Tegan had given him to Alice herself. She'd seen her with Monkey.

'This isn't supposed to happen,' Tegan shouted, her fists clenched and her voice lost to the droning engines above. Then she heard Alice's faint and childish voice drift back to her as she ran. 'I've dropped him.'

Tegan suddenly realized how stupid she'd been to give Monkey back to Alice. Maybe this is what happened before. Maybe Alice *had* taken Monkey out with her. But she'd dropped him. Somewhere in between the house and the shelter she'd dropped him.

Tegan glanced towards the shelter. Chrissie and her mother were still running towards it.

Nobody had noticed that Alice, or she, were missing. Tegan floundered. She had never thought that this could happen.

'Chrissssiee . . . ' she screamed. But neither Chrissie nor her mother heard. There was too much confusion. Too much noise. Too much darkness. Tegan waited for their heads to turn around, but neither did.

She would have to go back for Alice. There was nothing else she could do. Tegan couldn't watch her run towards the house, knowing what was going to happen. 'Alice,' Tegan tried to scream, but it came out as no more than a hoarse whisper.

'Alice,' she tried again. But Alice had gone too far to hear.

Tegan started to run. Her legs felt like lead, but she willed them to work. Her eyes were set on Alice, her brown pig-tails bobbing up and down as she ran down the garden. The planes droned overhead. Tegan felt as though they were chasing her just like she was chasing Alice. The whine of their engines was all Tegan could now hear. And all she could feel was the pounding of her own heart. But Tegan was making up ground. Alice's legs were not very long and couldn't compete with Tegan's.

Tegan was within touching distance. She stretched out her arm to Alice, but narrowly missed her shoulder. Two more strides and she would overtake her. Tegan pushed the last remaining energy out of her limbs and drew level.

'Monkey,' said Alice breathlessly. But the word was lost as Tegan grasped her by the wrists and half pulled, half fell with her, on to the wet earth. As they crashed to the ground a plane swept low over their heads. Tegan felt if she were to stand up she would be able to touch it. Seconds later as she lay, half on top of Alice, the bomb exploded.

For a second, Tegan didn't know if she was dead or alive. The sound was deafening and was immediately followed by vibrating earth beneath her and swirling dust above her. Tegan lay where she was, not daring to move or breathe. Alice lay just as still beneath her.

CHAPTER 17

Monkey

All that had happened yesterday. 'Was it really only yesterday?' thought Tegan as she stared down at the black and white photograph in her hands. Its frame lay on the bedroom floor where she sat. She cast her mind back. Things had happened so fast after the bomb landed.

Tegan could remember somebody coming up to them. It had been an adult, who had half dragged them back to the shelter. Tegan had clung to Alice, her fingernails digging into the woollen material of Alice's winter coat. Tegan wouldn't let go.

One minute there had been dust and noise, confusion and people shouting. Tegan thought she had heard Chrissie's mum's voice crying out Alice's name. Then the next minute, as she had stumbled down the steps and into the shelter, she had felt the mask back on her face. Without stopping to think, she had pulled it off and found herself instantly back in the garden shed.

Tegan was alone and back in the present. She was slumped on to the floor, gasping for breath. How would she find out now if Alice had survived?

Tegan had spent several minutes brushing the dust from her clothes and piecing her thoughts together. As she ventured back out into the garden, with the gas mask box in her hand, Tegan had met Nanna. She'd had a big smile on her face and her arms were outstretched. 'Good news,' she'd called. 'You've got a baby brother. His name is Kit. And Mum is fine.' And with that she had taken Tegan into her arms and hugged her.

Dad had come and collected her yesterday. He said that Mum would be out of hospital early tomorrow and she wanted them all to be together when she came home with Kit. Tegan had had to pack quickly and there had been no time to mention Alice to Nanna. No time even to see if there were any clues as to whether she was alive. It had all been such a rush. There had been hurried goodbyes and then she and Dad had driven straight back home.

Tegan had sat with the gas mask box on her lap for the entire journey.

'What's that?' Dad had asked.

'A present from Nanna,' said Tegan. 'A very special present.'

Suddenly, Tegan had felt as though she had been catapulted into another world. It was her own world, but she wasn't sure that she had quite finished with the one she was leaving behind.

Tegan slept in the car on the journey home. She could just about remember Dad carrying her into the house, but that was all. 'You're home now,' he had said. Everything had suddenly felt as if it were all a part of a dream.

She remembered letting the feeling wash over

her as she fell into a deep sleep.

* * *

Tegan put the picture back into its frame. There was definitely another girl in the photo. 'But maybe I just never noticed her before,' thought Tegan. 'Maybe it's not Alice, but just another girl on the beach, accidentally caught in the picture.'

Dad poked his head around the door.

'Are you coming down for some breakfast?' he asked.

'Yep,' said Tegan getting to her feet.

As Dad's head disappeared back around the door, Tegan called out to him.

'Dad,' she said.

Her father came back into the doorway.

'I've been thinking,' said Tegan. 'I think I'd like to give Kit something. A present, just from me. But I don't know what.'

Tegan's father smiled and he thought for a moment or two.

'Well,' he said slowly. 'You know what you

could give him?'

'What?' said Tegan. She had no idea what he was about to suggest.

'You could give him the monkey that Auntie Alice gave you when you were born. I'm sure she'd be very proud to hear that you had passed him on.'

Tegan followed the gaze of her father's eyes to the bookshelves behind her head. There, sitting in front of a pile of books was Monkey. Tegan thought he looked as though he had been living there for years. 'I suppose he has,' she thought to herself. He was a little more ragged than when Tegan had last seen him in Alice's arms. But it was definitely Monkey.

'What a good idea,' she said turning back to her dad. Then she smiled.

'Come on,' she said. 'I'm starving. Let's go and have breakfast.'

About the author

I started out as a stage manager with a Theatre-in-Education company, touring schools in a battered old van. Later, I worked for BBC television, where I worked on children's programmes, including *Grange Hill*. Then I switched completely, to a writing career and I am now the editor of *Girl Talk* magazine.

I've always been interested in the years surrounding the Second World War. My parents were children then and I love hearing their stories. The idea for *The War Monkey* was in my head for two years before I actually wrote it!